The REALLY ROTTEN Princess

and the Cupcake Catastrophe

by Lady Cecily Snodgrass
illustrated by Mike Lester

Ready-to-Read

Simon Spotlight
New York   London   Toronto   Sydney   New Delhi

SIMON SPOTLIGHT
An imprint of Simon & Schuster Children's Publishing Division
1230 Avenue of the Americas, New York, New York 10020
Copyright © 2013 by Simon & Schuster, Inc.
For information about special discounts for bulk purchases, please contact Simon & Schuster
Special Sales at 1-866-506-1949 or business@simonandschuster.com.
The Simon & Schuster Speakers Bureau can bring authors to your live event. For more information
or to book an event contact the Simon & Schuster Speakers Bureau at 1-866-248-3049 or visit our
website at www.simonspeakers.com.
Manufactured in the United States of America 0813 LAK
First Edition
10 9 8 7 6 5 4 3 2 1
Library of Congress Cataloging-in-Publication Data
Snodgrass, Cecily.
The really rotten princess and the cupcake catastrophe / by Lady Cecily Snodgrass ; illustrated by
Mike Lester. — First edition.
pages cm
Summary: "The princesses at Miss Prunerot's school are planning a bake sale featuring Regina's
special cupcakes. Regina can't resist the temptation to live up to her nickname and do something
really rotten to ruin everything"—Provided by publisher.
[1. Princesses—Fiction. 2. Behavior—Fiction. 3. Cupcakes—Fiction. 4. Schools—Fiction.] I. Lester,
Mike, illustrator. II. Title.
PZ7.S68032Rf 2013
[E]—dc23
2012046165
ISBN 978-1-4424-8973-8 (pbk)
ISBN 978-1-4424-8974-5 (hc)
ISBN 978-1-4424-8975-2 (eBook)

Regina was being punished. The Royal Unicorn Stable was a mess, and it was her job to clean it up.

But in spite of this nasty task, she was happy.

The other princesses were calling
her the Really Rotten Princess,
and she *loved* the name. Now she
just had to live up to it.

The next day in class,
Miss Prunerot was giving
a lesson on the best way
to capture the heart of a prince.

After all, it was a rule
that every princess must
someday find her prince.

But Miss Prunerot said they were all wrong.

She informed them that there was only one sure way to capture a prince's heart.

AND HERE IS OUR TEXTBOOK!

Recipes to Bag a Prince

Miss Prunerot passed out the books, and each princess chose a recipe to make.

Princess Dragonbreath made s'mores.

WITH TOASTED MARSHMALLOWS!

Princess Sweet Pea built a ten-layer sponge cake.

And after putting on a hairnet, Princess Lovelylocks began braiding a loaf of challah.

HE'LL LOVE HOW EAGER I AM TO GET MARRIED.

Princess Wishlicious went right to making a wedding cake.

Meanwhile Princess Seafoam decorated her doughnuts with a nautical theme.

ONCE YOU'VE CAUGHT THEM, TRAINING THEM IS EASY!

Miss Prunerot was already looking forward to next week's lesson.

Regina's first thought was to make something disgusting.

But she knew everyone would expect that.

So instead she baked the yummiest-looking cupcakes that anyone had ever seen. They were perfect!

At first no one wanted to taste them. Then Princess Somnambula woke up and took a nibble.

Even Mrs. Prunerot took a small taste.

The thought of money
got Miss Prunerot's attention.
After all, kings and queens hardly
ever pay their tuition bills.

Then Princess Wishlicious had an idea.

Miss Prunerot thought
it was a wonderful plan.
The princesses all agreed.

Regina was happy to share her recipe. Only no one noticed that she made one change at the end.

The next day, at the wizard's convention, the cupcakes were put out on display.

The wizards came out of their first meeting, and they were very hungry.

As they lined up to buy cupcakes, one of them recognized Regina. It was her parents' court wizard, Maldemar.

Maldemar knew she was up to no good. He tried to stop the other wizards from eating the cupcakes, but he was too late.

Don't eat them! She's rotten!

And when wizards get sick, all sorts of things can go wrong.

Magic spells flew this way and that as the wizards lost control.

Princess Wishlicious ended up with a zipper where her mouth had been . . .

GLP!

. . . while Princess Seafoam was turned into an oyster.

Princess Dragonbreath could suddenly belch fire!

Princess Somnambula was transformed into an alarm clock.

And Princess Sweet Pea turned a bright green color.

OooHH!

Princess Lovelylocks knew something about her had been changed, but wasn't sure what.

Luckily, Maldemar was okay.
With a wave of his wand,
he changed the
princesses back into
their old selves. . . .

MY HAIR!

IS IT TIME
TO GET UP?

PTTUUI.

. . . whether they wanted
to be or not.

Maldemar knew full well who had caused this mess . . . and he knew just how to punish her for her dire deeds.

Raising his wand high, the wizard
pointed it at Regina . . .

. . . and transformed her into
the tastiest-looking cupcake ever.
The perfect punishment for a
really, really rotten princess.